My Working Mom

by Peter Glassman

illustrated by Tedd Arnold

Morrow Junior Books

New York

For Sandra Glassman,
my very own working mom
—P.G.

For D. R. M.
—T.A.

Watercolors and colored pencils were used for the full-color artwork.
The text type is 23.75-point Galliard.

Text copyright © 1994 by Peter Glassman
Illustrations copyright © 1994 by Tedd Arnold
All rights reserved. No part of this book may be reproduced or utilized in any form or by any means,
electronic or mechanical, including photocopying, recording, or by any information storage and
retrieval system, without permission in writing from the Publisher. Inquiries should be addressed to
William Morrow and Company, Inc., 1350 Avenue of the Americas, New York, NY 10019.
Printed in Singapore at Tien Wah Press.
3 4 5 6 7 8 9 10
Library of Congress Cataloging-in-Publication Data
Glassman, Peter J. My working Mom / by Peter Glassman ; illustrated by Tedd Arnold. p. cm. Summary:
Although she sometimes resents her mother's work as a witch, a young girl decides to keep her mother just the
way she is. ISBN 0-688-12259-0 (trade). — ISBN 0-688-12260-4 (library) [1. Working mothers—Fiction.
2. Mothers and daughters—Fiction. 3. Witches—Fiction.] I. Arnold, Tedd, ill. II. Title. PZ7.G481438My
1994 [E]—dc20 93-22036 CIP AC

It isn't easy having a working mom.

Especially when she
enjoys her work.

If Mom isn't busy in her lab,
she's flying off to a meeting somewhere.

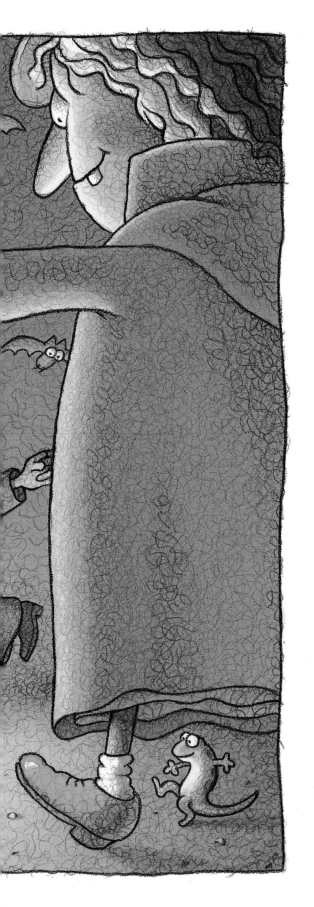

Mom says her
meetings are boring,
but I'll bet they're a blast!

Of course, sometimes
Mom's work doesn't go
quite the way she planned.

And when Mom's had a bad day at work— watch out!

Sometimes I think Mom likes her job more than being a mom, especially when she makes one of her weird dinners.

Or yells at me for playing
with something she's working on.

Still, Mom always gives me
the greatest birthday parties.
And she never forgets
to make me a cake that is
out of this world!

If I'm in the school play,
I can count on Mom to be there—
even if she does usually arrive
at the last moment.

And when my team is playing,
no one cheers louder than Mom!

One day my teacher asked our parents to come to school and talk about their jobs.

Some of the parents were sort of dull,
a few were kind of creepy.

But not *my* mom!
All the kids thought
she was great!

Even though I don't always like having a working mom, I just can't picture mine any other way.

So I guess if I had to choose,
I'd keep my mom just the way she is.

A
JACQUES LOWE
VISUAL ARTS PROJECTS
BOOK

Book design by Joseph Guglietti.   Jacket design by Anne Shannon.

Typeset in Cochin and Gill Sans.   Printed in Hong Kong.

LIBRARY OF CONGRESS CATALOGING-IN-PUBLICATION DATA
Coleman, A.D.
Looking at photographs–animals/photographs compiled by Jacques Lowe;
text and captions by A.D. Coleman
48p.   21.6 x 28 cm.   Includes index.
ISBN 0-8118-0418-6
1. Photography of animals—Juvenile literature, 2. Photography, Artistic—
Juvenile literature [1. Photography of animals. 2. Photography, Artistic]
I. Lowe, Jacques.   II. Title.
TR727.C65 1995
778.9'32–dc 20   94–10109
CIP
AC

Distributed in Canada by Raincoast Books
8680 Cambie Street, Vancouver, B.C. V6P 6M9

10 9 8 7 6 5 4 3 2 1

Chronicle Books
275 Fifth Street
San Francisco, California 94103

Animals

Written by
A.D. Coleman

Series Editor
Jacques Lowe

Chronicle Books ⌖ San Francisco

Jacques Lowe, TAKING AIM AT THE BIRD

Introduction

The invention of photography in the nineteenth century was something like solving a jig-saw puzzle. Many of the pieces—such as the camera, and the lens, and the knowledge that exposure to light affected some materials—had been in place for centuries. The first permanent photograph was made in 1826 by Nicephore Niepce. However, not until 1839 did a Frenchman, L. J. M. Daguerre, and an Englishman, W. H. Fox Talbot, announce to the public two methods for making photographs. Ever since, photography has been changing the way we see our world. One example is what photography has shown us about animals. Some of the very first images ever made by humans, the prehistoric cave paintings, are pictures of animals. So it was only to be expected that photographers would use their medium to look at the various kinds of creatures that share this planet with us.

Painters, etchers, and other graphic artists were limited in their ability to observe and represent animals in motion, and in the wild, or under water. And in the early days of photography, the large, heavy cameras and long exposures that were necessary restricted photographers in much the same way. By experimenting, some of them, like Eadweard Muybridge in his studies of "animal locomotion," found ways of overcoming those obstacles. Since then, cameras have become lighter and films much faster. Today, in combination with other scientific advances, photography makes it possible to study and depict the details of animal life in almost any habitat: how they raise their young, find their food, and protect their territory, among other activities. These photographs show us things about tame and wild animals that we were never able to see before.

Over the past century and a half, photographers have made pictures of thousands of different kinds of animals around the world. Within these pages, you'll find underwater photography by David Doubilet, a microscopic study of a flea by David Scharf, action pictures of a housecat by Tony Mendoza, and portraits by Mary Ellen Mark.

But this book isn't just about animals; it is about photography. And understanding photographs is an important skill. This book will help you learn about how photographs are made, what they have to tell us, and how we can get the most out of looking at them carefully. You can apply the ideas you'll find here not only to pictures of animals, but to the many different kinds of photographs that come into your life every day. We hope that it will change the way you look at and think about all photographs.

MULE, 1885
Eadweard Muybridge, British-American

There is much in the visible world that can't be seen with the "naked eye." Photography has allowed us to observe and understand some of those things in new ways. One of the subjects that it has helped us to analyze is motion.

There are many ways to depict motion in photographs. One of them is by making pictures that stop or "freeze" things as they are moving. Eadweard Muybridge invented a complex system for doing just that. He arranged a group of cameras in a line, alongside a track, timed to go off one after another. Then he let various animals (and people, too) move down that track. The cameras made their *exposures* as the *subjects* moved along. When the resulting images were developed, printed, and lined up, they formed a *photographic sequence* that cut that motion into separate moments. For the first time, people were able to examine the different stages that are part of any movement. So these images have helped painters to depict human and animal motion more accurately. They have allowed scientists and doctors to study the ways in which human and animal bodies function.

This mule walking is an example of Muybridge's work. It looks very much like a strip of movie film. As a matter of fact, his experiments led directly to the invention of *motion pictures*. If you want to see how, you can try an experiment yourself. Make a photocopy of this series of pictures. Then cut out each one and stack them up, keeping them in their original order. Staple the stack on the left-hand side. You've just made a "flip book." Flip through the pages quickly, front to back, and you'll see the mule come to life.

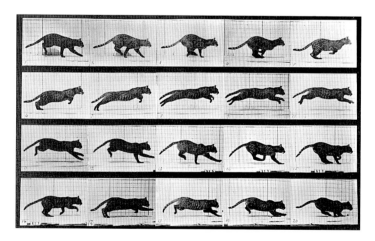

Eadweard Muybridge, COUGAR
Muybridge's experiments with movement ranged from people to animals in action, including wild creatures like this cougar.

THE TERMINAL, 1893
Alfred Stieglitz, American

When Alfred Stieglitz went out to make this picture one snowy winter day more than a century ago, he was putting his abilities as a photographer, and his equipment, to a test. He was using a brand new invention: a small, portable *hand camera*.

The cameras that professional photographers used in those days were big, and so heavy that they had to be held steady by a *tripod*. But few photographers at that time would have tried to work under snowy conditions with any camera, much less with one thought of as a toy. Stieglitz knew that the cold weather could freeze his little camera and his film, and that the *available light* he'd be working with was dim. Light is the photographer's basic raw material, a necessary ingredient in the picture-making process, and there wasn't much of it that day.

Arthur Elgort, RODEO

This picture of a working horse is quite different from the one opposite; Stieglitz needed long exposures, Elgort uses high speed to capture this dramatic moment.

In New York City at the turn of the century, public transportation was provided by horse-drawn carriages. When the photographer came to the terminal at the beginning of the line, he found a scene that excited him. There were the carriages, being cleaned out for the next run. There was the terminal watchman, checking the horses. And there were the hard-working horses themselves. The sweat from their bodies was turning into steam in the cold air.

It was so dark out that Stieglitz knew his film wouldn't register all the details his eye could see. But he believed that he'd be able to reveal just enough so that we'd understand what we were looking at. The darkness of the resulting image captures the mood and atmosphere of that moment: the feeling of hard work being done without complaint, under difficult conditions.

Stieglitz's test was a success. He turned the limitations of his film and the light conditions to his own advantage, and proved that even a "toy" camera could be used to make a powerful image. Taking risks and experimenting with new tools and materials is one of the ways in which photographers, like other artists, stretch the boundaries of their medium.

M. FOLLETETE TEACHING HIS DOG TUPY TO JUMP OVER A BROOK, 1912
Jacques-Henri Lartigue, French

This photograph was made by an eighteen-year-old named Jacques-Henri Lartigue. When he grew up, he became a famous photographer and painter. But many of the best photographs he made were the ones he created around 1900 during his childhood in France.

Many families have scrapbooks in which they organize snapshots, graduation portraits, and other personal photographs. These pictures of Lartigue's started out as just that kind of family album photography. Lartigue was too small to take part in a lot of his family's activities, so his parents bought him a camera. It was a big, heavy wooden one that he had to support on a *tripod*. He had to learn to develop his own *negatives* and print his pictures himself. With his camera, instead of just being a spectator watching from the sidelines, Lartigue became his family's historian, making the images that recorded their everyday experiences. And one of the reasons those pictures are important today is that they let us see how a typical upper class French family lived almost a century ago.

This picture also shows us how photography can be used to stop or "freeze" motion. Lartigue waited until the exact moment that this dog was released from the hands of his father's secretary, and then opened the *shutter* of his camera and made the *exposure* on the film. This action only lasted for a split second. Yet the dog and the man are as still as statues, and, in this photograph, they'll stay in that position forever.

Jacques-Henri Lartigue, DEEK OUR AFGHAN
With the sun behind his subject, Lartigue used backlighting *to outline Deek, the family's* Afghan hound.

CAT WITH KITTEN CROSSING STREET, circa 1925
Harry Warnecke, American

The man who made this picture was a *press photographer*, making images for publication in newspapers and magazines. The way the shadows fall suggests that this scene took place about noon on a bright, sunny day. From the clothing worn by the people in the crowd, the policeman's uniform, and the cars, we can guess that it was made some time in the 1920s. But it's easy to tell what the photograph is about.

All the people we can see in this scene—the officer and the onlookers—are men. The photographer was close to the action and visible to everyone; in fact, quite a few of the men on the left seem to be looking in the photographer's direction. But the real focus of attention at this moment is a mother cat carrying her kitten across the street.

André Kertész, RUE BOURGEOIS
Unlike the attention paid to the cat crossing the street with her young, this old woman crossing a street with many cats is ignored. One is a news photo, this one a normal, everyday event.

She, her kitten, and a big car occupy the center of the *frame*; positioning something in the middle of the picture is one way photographers let us know what to look at first.

It is very dangerous for animals to cross city streets. But this car, and, in fact, all the automobiles we can see are standing still at the policeman's command because this is a mother with her baby, and one of our society's beliefs is that mothers and babies deserve special protection, even if they're cats, and even if it means stopping traffic at midday on a busy city avenue.

We usually think of press photographers as people who cover important, newsworthy events, such as crimes, elections, accidents, demonstrations, and the activities of important people. But these photographers are also always on the lookout for those little moments in everyday life that tell us something about the way that average people behave. Such pictures, which are called "human interest," are often humorous, like this one. They help to remind us that minor events are an important part of the texture of our lives. Warnecke's photograph, which was made in New York, suggests that the big city isn't all that cold and impersonal; even on a busy day, people still stop to watch and protect a stray cat and her kitten.

SEA LION, 1959
Hiroshi Hamaya, Japanese

A *likeness* is any image that resembles a person. A *portrait* is a picture that suggests something about that particular individual's personality. Animals have identities, habits, moods, emotions, and expressions just as humans do, and photographers often find ways of revealing those characteristics. That's what Hiroshi Hamaya, a Japanese photographer, does in this image.

Most portraits are *close-up* views of their subjects; that way, the details of the subjects' appearances and expressions can be seen. So Hamaya used a *telephoto lens,* which works like a telescope, to give us the impression of being very close to this sea lion.

He waited until only the sea lion's head and neck were above water and visible to him. This has the effect of *vignetting* or isolating those parts; and the sea lion's head and neck fill most of the space within the picture's *frame.* These methods are traditions in the craft of photographic portraiture.

The position of the sea lion's head is what a portrait photographer would call *three-quarter profile*: we're seeing it mostly from the side. This lets us notice its eye, mouth, ear, nose, and whiskers, as well as the shape of its head. Studying its facial features also makes us think about this sea lion as a unique creature.

But above all, what makes this feel like a portrait is the expression that Hamaya captured on the sea lion's face. It's a calm, satisfied look, and, in combination with its closed eyes, uplifted head, and motionless pose, it makes it seem as if the sea lion is thinking, or daydreaming, or remembering. Hamaya chose to show this animal at a moment when it seems to be doing something humans do as well; that helps us to identify with it.

Susan Middleton, PEREGRINE FALCON
While the sea lion is caught in his natural habitat, this bird of prey, photographed in a studio, looks directly at the camera in the same way a human being sitting for a portrait might.

13

UNTITLED, NEW YORK, circa 1961
Garry Winogrand, American

Painters, who start with a blank canvas, have to choose what to put into their pictures. But photographers, who begin by pointing their cameras at something in the real world, have to decide what to leave out.

Photographers refer to the edges of the photographic image as the *frame*. The act of deciding where that border will be placed, in order to select a section of whatever's in front of the camera and to leave out the rest of the scene, is called *framing*. It's one of the most important decisions involved in making a photograph.

This photograph shows us a very common sight: a man feeding something, probably crackerjack or peanuts, to an elephant. But Garry Winogrand tells us what's happening by showing us just a few bits of information. We don't see the whole elephant; only its trunk, stretching out from the left edge of the frame. And we don't see the man, either; there's nothing visible except his right hand and forearm, reaching forward from the other side of the image. These two extensions form a horizontal line, dividing the photograph almost exactly in half. This creates a very balanced *composition*, while at the same time conveying a sense of action; we can feel the coordinated motions of these two separate creatures.

Sylvia Plachy, RHINO VIDEO
Unlike Winogrand's photograph, Sylvia Plachy's picture emphasizes the differences between human and animal activities.

Winogrand waited for the precise instant in which their behavior would reveal its purpose. Some photographers call this the *decisive moment*. The tip of the elephant's trunk is turned upwards, in its characteristic position for receiving something; the man's hand is opening in the way a hand does when it's releasing something. Even if we couldn't see something dropping from it, we'd know just what basic act of friendly sharing was going on.

14

ELEPHANTS IN AFRICA, 1963
Peter Beard, American

At first glance, Peter Beard's photo of a herd of African elephants seems like a random, abstract pattern of dark shapes on a light background. Once we look closely, however, we can pick out smaller groups within the herd: families, groups of older elephants, and even a few baby elephants holding their mothers' tails with their trunks.

Because we know how large an elephant is, and because we can see so many of them here, we know something about this photograph: it had to have been made from quite a distance. The angle from which the photographer is observing these creatures and the few other objects in the scene, like the tree in the upper right-hand corner, tells us that the photographer is high above the herd. He's much higher than he'd be if he were standing on a tall ladder, or even sitting in a treetop. In fact, if his feet were on the ground, he'd need to be standing on a mountain to get this different perspective, which is often called a *bird's-eye view*. But there aren't many mountains that high on the African plains, which are mostly flat. To get this viewpoint, Beard had to have a pilot fly him over the herd while he made his picture. The airplane could probably have gone even higher, but the higher he would get, the harder it would be for the viewer to recognize the *subjects* of the image, and to see any details.

The photographer may have chosen to make his *exposure* at this distance because if the plane got much closer, it might have scared the elephants into stampeding. In any case, his decision had an impact on the feeling that this picture gives us. By showing us only part of the herd and not letting us see its edges, he suggests that this herd is so large that even an *aerial*

Jonathan Blair, CROCODILE EATING FROG
This close-up photo of a frog being snatched by a crocodile shows us clearly what wildlife is like, something we can only guess at in the opposite photo. Will this crocodile get to eat this frog, or will the frog, hanging on for dear life, be able to escape? That is left a mystery.

photograph like this can't contain it. The bits and pieces of other elephants that we see walking into and out of the frame tell us that there are more elephants here than we've been shown. Beard leaves it to us to imagine how many more there might be. Photographing from airplanes or hot air balloons is known as *aerial photography*. It's a technique that began to be used almost immediately after the invention of photography. Now it's taken for granted, but when it first started it showed people the world from above, which was a *viewpoint* no one had ever experienced before.

PICNIC AT GLYNDEBOURNE, 1967
Tony Ray-Jones, English

This photograph is about the opposite of curiosity: taking things for granted. The English photographer, Tony Ray-Jones, was interested in the way people from his country behave in various situations. At an opera festival, he came across this couple sitting down to a picnic lunch. He decided to make a picture of what at first glance looks like an ordinary scene.

But the result is a photograph that tells us a lot about the people in it. One of its themes is their sense of order. Everything about this couple and their location is very organized. The lawn they are sitting on is carefully mowed. The line where it meets the field is perfectly straight. Their table and chairs and picnic basket are placed neatly. The man has hung his suit jacket carefully over the back of his chair. They are even both dressed in formal evening clothes in a situation where most people would wear ordinary street clothes.

But there's more here. Where the lawn ends, a field starts — a field in which half a dozen cows and several dozen sheep can be seen grazing. There's no wall or fence between the lawn and the field. But the humans are clearly on one side, and the animals on the other.

What makes this situation even funnier is that none of these creatures is paying any attention to each other. The cattle are busy feeding, while the people are reading. Although the photographer is standing within speaking distance of the couple to make this photo, he is being ignored too. He's the only one who's not taking things for granted. Photographers learn to be close observers, to find the unexpected in the everyday world.

Jacques Lowe, HORSE IN COURTYARD
Here the horse is ignoring the photographer, who is studying the horse's white form in relation to the pale tones of the courtyard.

KENTUCKY DERBY MORNING, 1972
Jacques Lowe, American

Photography is a medium that can be used in many ways. Whatever the subject matter may be, the photographer usually has a variety of approaches from which to choose. We've seen how Eadweard Muybridge used still photographs to *analyze* motion; a still photograph can also convey the *feeling* of motion. That's the case with this picture of a racehorse and its rider.

The photographer was standing at the edge of the track when this jockey and horse passed him. While he knew ahead of time that they'd be coming, he still only had time to make one exposure on his film. So he had to decide in advance how he wanted the picture to look.

Because his *subjects* would be moving so fast, he set his camera for a high *shutter speed*. Otherwise the horse and rider would have registered on the film only as an unrecognizable streak of color. He could have held his camera absolutely still, in which case his subjects would have appeared to be frozen in mid-step. But he wanted the photo to give us the sensation of speed. So as the horse and jockey came past, he *centered* them in the *viewfinder* and *panned* his camera, following their movement with the lens.

This panning had the effect of blurring those parts of the scene that weren't moving—the grass, the dirt of the track, the fences—in the *foreground* and *background* of the image. That's the way things appear to us when *we're* moving past them very quickly. The horse and rider are in the *middle ground*, and in this photograph they are a bit blurry, but we can still see immediately what they are. That's how things look when they pass us at high speed. So this picture really captures the experience of rapid movement from two perspectives: from the rider's point of view, and from the spectator's.

Jacques Lowe, HORSE RACE
Here the photographer shows us the same horse on the same day, racing in the Kentucky Derby, but lets us see it from a very different perspective: a worm's-eye view.

NEW YORK, 1974, 1974
Elliott Erwitt, American

This funny photograph is about being small—*very* small—in relation to other living things. The little dog looking right at the camera is all dressed up in a hat and sweater. It's surrounded by three other creatures who are much, much bigger: a Great Dane, a woman (probably the owner of both dogs), and the photographer who made this picture.

It looks as if the woman and her pets were out for a walk on a chilly day. If Elliott Erwitt had taken the photograph while standing up, all he would have been able to see of the chihuahua would have been its back. Obviously Erwitt didn't think that was a very interesting picture, because you couldn't see the little dog's face, and because you couldn't see its size in relationship to the size of its companions. This relationship between sizes is called *scale.* Big differences in scale can be surprising, which is what makes this picture so funny.

An important aspect of this picture is that Erwitt made it from an unusual *point of view.* The photographer's eye is usually looking through the *viewfinder,* the small opening that lets the photographer see what the lens is pointing at. It's possible that Erwitt just put his camera down on the sidewalk and pressed the *shutter release.* But it's also possible that he lay down on the street to see what the picture would look like and to be sure that the *lens,* the eye of the camera, was pointed accurately to catch the image he had in mind. One question that's important to ask when looking at any photograph is this: where did the photographer have to be in order to make the picture?

Anonymous, LITTLE GIRL WITH SAINT BERNARD   *This photograph, made around 1900, reverses the sense of the opposite picture; the Saint Bernard dog is bigger than the little girl.*

ERNIE WITH DRAGONFLY, 1985
Antonio "Tony" Mendoza, Cuban-American

Photographers are like cats. They observe everything around them and they think like hunters, following their instincts, always preparing to pounce. (It's no accident that the word *snapshot*, used to describe photos made very quickly, is a term used by hunters as well.)

This picture by Tony Mendoza is about hunting. Ernie, the cat, is chasing a dragonfly. He's in the middle of swinging a paw, trying to catch this tiny insect. If we follow his eyes, we can see that his attention is fixed on the bug as it speeds away from him. We can also see, from the distance between them, that Ernie missed; the dragonfly was too fast for him. All this was happening very quickly; an attachment on the camera called a *flash* provided a quick burst of bright light to freeze this action on film.

Tony Mendoza, UNTITLED, *from the* Leela *series*
In this photo, Mendoza hints at something terrible about to happen, and so evokes our sense of anticipation. Will the dog Leela touch the ant? What will happen if she does?

But there's another kind of hunting going on in this picture as well. While Ernie was stalking the dragonfly, a photographer was stalking Ernie. As you can see, the photograph was made from what photographers call Ernie's *eye level*. A cat's eye level is usually between six and ten inches above the ground. A grown-up's eye level, when standing, averages between five and six feet above the ground. What's your eye level?

To make this picture, the photographer had to change from his eye level to Ernie's; he had to get down on his hands and knees, or lie on his stomach. So even though we can't see the photographer crawling around on the floor with his camera, the photograph lets us know that that is how this picture was created. Photographs often tell us as much about how the photograph was made as they do about the subject of the picture.

LEAFY SEA DRAGON, 1985
David Doubilet, American

A painter can paint an animal from his or her imagination, from memory, from a photograph, or directly from life. A photographer doesn't have all those choices. To photograph an animal, or anything else, the camera has to be where the *subject* is.

Sometimes the photographer can bring the subject home, or to the studio, or someplace else that's convenient. But many subjects can't be transported. And one thing that photography does very well is to show us how things look where they live, in their natural environment. Photographers don't just think about the objects, animals, and people they're looking at. They often try to show us the *context* in which those subjects exist.

David Doubilet, who made this magical image of a sea horse, specializes in underwater photography. He puts on scuba gear and uses specially designed waterproof camera equipment to make his pictures of the creatures who live in the ocean. This one lets us get a look at this sea horse in motion. When he made the photograph, Doubilet was actually below the sea horse in the water; we can tell that because behind and above this little animal we can see a bit of daylight at the water's surface.

Bob Talbot, DOLPHINS

The light in this underwater photo is very mysterious. We can recognize these silhouetted figures as dolphins, even without seeing the details of their bodies.

David Doubilet used a kind of flash attachment called a *strobe* to illuminate the sea horse. If he'd depended on the natural light, all we would have seen is a *silhouette* of this beautiful creature. Because of the strobe, we can also see the details of the sea horse's body, and its brilliant orange-yellow-green colors. Experienced photographers learn to anticipate the situations in which they'll be working, and choose equipment that's suited to those conditions.

EN ATTENDANT RALPH GIBSON, 1986
Lionel Deriaz, Swiss

The first decision a photographer makes about what's going to be included in a picture happens at the moment of exposure, when the button that lets light through the camera's lens is pressed. But he or she has another chance to select from what that light has registered on the *film*. This opportunity comes when the *negative* or *slide* is being used to make a *print*. At that point, a photographer can choose to show only a portion of the image on the negative. This process is called *cropping*.

This image is narrower from top to bottom than any standard negative. From its proportions, we can tell that we're not seeing everything that was in the negative from which the image was printed. That tells us that in making the print, Lionel Deriaz cropped his negative to produce this long, narrow rectangle. This allowed him to organize the *composition* of his picture very precisely, so that something pulls our eyes toward all four edges of the image at once.

Ralph Gibson, SWAN
The young disciple's photo opposite is based on this image by the master. Photographers often build on images they admire by other photographers even when, as in this case, they live on different continents.

At the far left, the swan's tail almost touches the border of the picture. On the far right, ripples reach that edge of the image, telling us that the swan has just ducked its head, perhaps looking for a fish in the pond. We don't actually see the swan's head; along with part of its neck, that's been cropped out. But we do see the reflection of its head and neck, in *silhouette*, in the water beneath its body. There, the top of its head, upside down, almost touches the bottom edge of the picture. So we get the impression of seeing a complete swan, but we have to put the pieces of it together, like solving a jigsaw puzzle. Sometimes it takes work to make sense of a photograph, just as it does to understand a story or a poem; but the best photographs are worth the effort.

FLEA, 1986
David Scharf, American

Photographers pay attention to little things as well as big ones. And some of them use photography to study objects so small that they can't be seen by the "naked eye."

This is a *close-up* picture of a live flea, viewed from the the front. Most of us have seen fleas, but even if we've looked at them closely, we can't have seen much more than little black spots with legs. Here we get to see all the extraordinary detail of its head and body. David Scharf, who specializes in microphotography, made this image using a camera attached to a scanning electron microscope which magnifies the subject, letting us see it many times larger than its actual size. He's made *microphotographs* of everything from bacteria and the cells of plants and animals to crystals and computer chips and a variety of what he calls "crawling life forms."

Ed Bridges, TERMITE IN AMBER
Because we know the average size of human fingers, this study of a termite trapped in amber gives us a sense of scale.

According to Scharf, the microscope he uses takes over a minute to scan its subject completely. If the subject is something motionless, like a crystal, this doesn't cause any problem. But if it's alive and capable of motion, like an insect, the process becomes much more difficult. "The mere heartbeat of a small animal can cause enough vibration of a limb to make photographing impractical, if not impossible," Scharf says. Imagine how hard it would be to photograph people if their heartbeats could ruin the picture. That gives some idea of the challenge Scharf faces when he works with these tiny creatures.

Aerial photography lets us look at the world from above, and *telephoto lenses* bring distant objects closer, so that we can see them in greater detail. *Microphotography* takes us into the marvelous, miniature world that's too small to see, making it possible for us to study the countless things that are so little that the eye can't observe them without assistance.

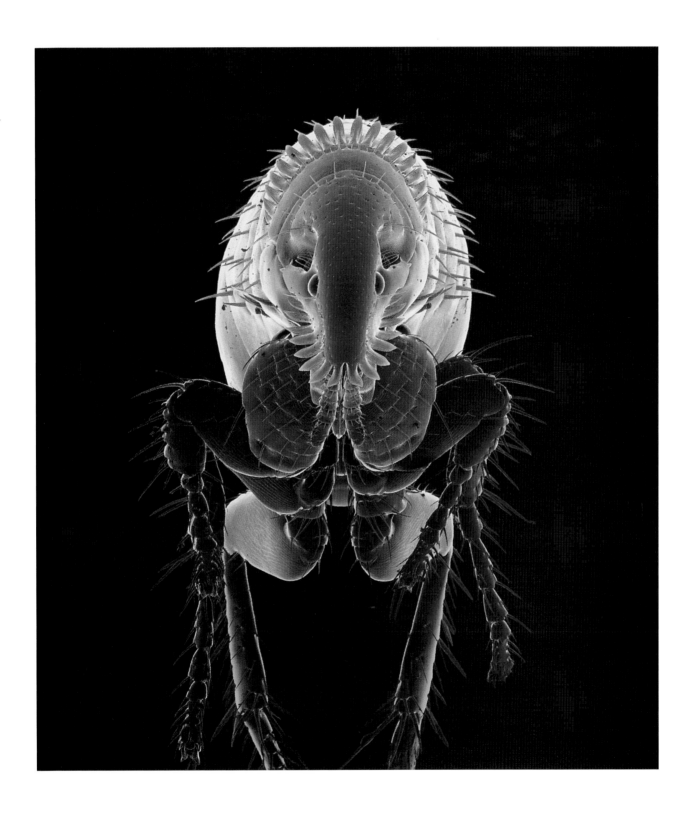

ROLLER ROVER, 1987
William Wegman, American

We tend to assume that photographs are facts, and that what they show us is always true. We think of photographers as people who show us the way events that really happened actually looked, without any interference from the person behind the camera. But, like all artists, photographers are capable of making things up and inventing stories. It's possible for photographers to create images based on their own imaginations. And sometimes what they imagine is very silly, and very funny.

Harry Whittier Frees, THE PRIDE OF THE SCHOOL   *In comparison with Wegman's accomplished dog, this cat's grumpy expression lets us imagine that it also can read and understand the insult on its cap.*

William Wegman didn't just happen to come across a dog wearing roller skates. This dog's name is Fay Ray, and she lives with Wegman. Somewhere along the line, Wegman discovered that Fay Ray liked posing for the camera. Once the photographer realized this, he began to invent all kinds of things for Fay Ray to do that would be unusual and funny to photograph. It was a way of playing for both of them.

To make this picture, Wegman and Fay Ray went into a *studio* in Manhattan where a special Polaroid camera is kept. Like a regular Polaroid camera, it shoots out a *color print* that *develops* in only a minute. The camera Wegman used in this studio works on the same principle, but it's as tall as a grown man. And the print that comes out of it is also very big: twenty inches by twenty-four inches.

To make this picture, Wegman helped Fay Ray get her paws into those skates. Then he told the dog to hold still, and the film was *exposed*. The picture shows us a dog that seems to be roller skating, but really it has more to do with make-believe and acting than it does with reporting the facts. Pictures like this teach us not to believe everything we see in photographs. They remind us that photography is a creative process.

GREAT INDIAN RHINOCEROS, 1989
James Balog, American

Like almost everything else we do, looking at the world can get to be a habit. When it does, we can end up looking at things without really seeing them, taking the world for granted instead of examining it carefully.

There's always more than one way to look at anything. The position from which a person looks at something is called a *viewpoint* or a *point of view*. And one of the ways photographers challenge our habits of seeing is by exploring different points of view.

Sometimes they startle us when they do this, because they've looked at something familiar from an angle we've forgotten about, or perhaps one we've never thought of before. But as we grow older, we develop our ability to understand what we see. And we also remember a lot of what we've seen during our lives. We may not be aware of how many ways we can recognize something until a glimpse of it from some unusual angle lets us identify it.

Bob Talbot, WHALE'S TAIL
This whale's tail also may not be instantly recognizable but in this case, the part is more familiar to us than the back of a rhino.

What happened when you first looked at this photograph? Did you realize immediately that it was a rhinoceros? If so, you've probably seen a rhino from behind, and could recognize it from these unexpected visual clues. Did it puzzle you until you read the picture's title? If so, you may never have seen the back end of a rhino. In any case, if you were asked to draw a rhinoceros, this probably isn't the way that you'd first think to represent it. This photo reminds us that there are always other possibilities to consider.

That's an extremely important lesson in photography. Looked at from an unexpected point of view, even the most ordinary subject can become truly surprising.

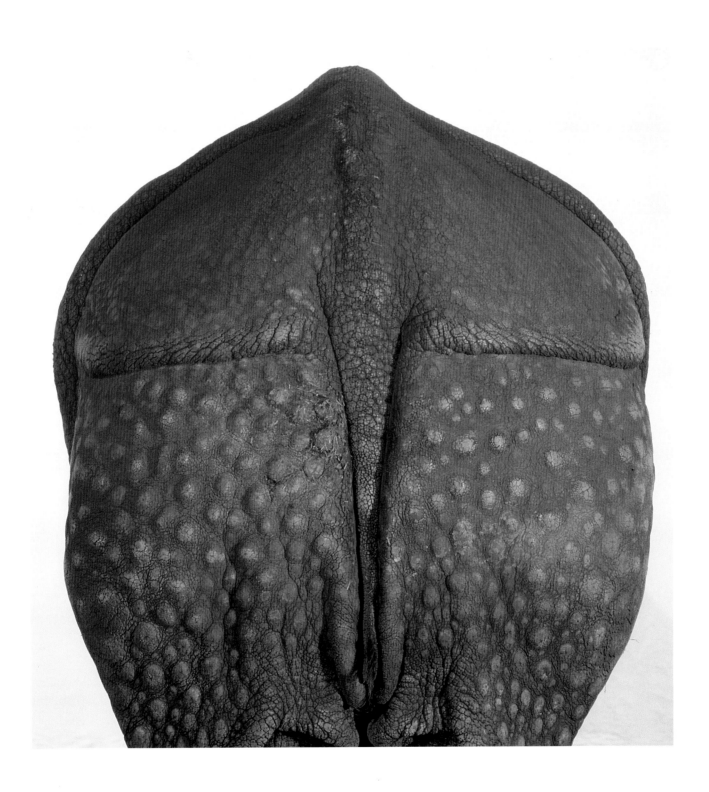

RAM PRAKASH SINGH WITH HIS ELEPHANT, SHYAMA,
Great Golden Circus, Ahmedabad, India, 1989
Mary Ellen Mark, American

One subject that photographers often explore is relationship: the connections between objects, between spaces and shapes, between animals, between people, and between the many possible combinations of all these things.

This picture is a *double portrait*, or a portrait of two creatures: a man who's an elephant trainer for a circus, and one of the elephants with which he works. They're both standing still and posing for the photographer, watching her; and, for that reason, it feels as if they're making eye contact with us. There's something particularly powerful about photographs in which people and animals appear to be looking us right in the eye.

Mary Ellen Mark spent many days getting to know the people and animals in this circus very well. She could have shown us many different aspects of the relationship between this man and elephant. She could have shown them practicing their act, or performing for an audience. But what she wanted to let us see was the emotional bond between two living beings who work, travel, and live together. From the photograph, we can tell that this particular relationship is based on friendship and trust.

Ram Prakash is standing very close to Shyama, which lets us see the difference in their proportions. Shyama is a full-grown elephant, much bigger than this man. Shyama's huge trunk is wrapped around Ram Prakash's neck. It's obvious that if Shyama wanted to hurt or even kill him, it would be easy for the elephant to do so. But there's no fear in Ram Prakash's gaze, even though he's not even carrying a whip, or a gun, or anything that could protect him from the elephant. So that big trunk, which could be dangerous, becomes this elephant's version of the arm that a bigger person might put around the shoulders of a smaller friend. And this photo becomes a study of friendship.

Mary Ellen Mark, HIPPO WITH TRAINER
The distance separating them makes the relationship between these two creatures seem much different — more formal, less loving.

EMPEROR PENGUINS AND CHICKS, 1992
Art Wolfe, American

Artists of all kinds often use their subject matter symbolically, to represent ideas, and photographers are no exception. One reason they so often observe animals is that animals do many things that remind us of aspects of human behavior.

For example, everything about this photograph says *family*. There are two adult penguins facing each other, leaning forward and pressing their foreheads together. They seem to be expressing affection for each other. At their feet are two young birds, probably their chicks. Each of these little creatures has nestled itself against one of its parents. They look very comfortable and secure there. These are all actions that we're familiar with in our daily lives; human families behave in much the same way.

The result is a photograph that looks a lot like the average family portrait: Mom and Dad and the kids, standing in a group, making a memento that shows their closeness and their love for each other. The penguins even look as if they dressed up for the occasion, since penguins always appear to be wearing tuxedos. The only difference is that these are penguins, not people. That is what makes this photograph surprising, as well as charming: it tells us something about ourselves by looking closely at something else.

Sometimes photographers find the subject matter that interests them close to home, but in other cases they have to travel to faraway places for it. To photograph these birds, Art Wolfe traveled all the way to the South Pole, the natural habitat of penguins. Perhaps that's one reason they seem so relaxed and fearless: they're right at home.

Robert Caputo, CHEETAH AND CUB, KENYA
Like the penguin photo, this study of a cheetah with its cub shows that photographers often pursue the same idea.

Glossary

AERIAL PHOTOGRAPHY: photography done from airplanes, balloons, or other aircraft

AVAILABLE LIGHT: whatever light is already present in the scene the photographer is observing, without the addition of flash or strobe

BACKGROUND: that part of the space in a scene or a photograph that's furthest from the camera

BACKLIGHTING: light that's coming from a source behind the subject

BIRD'S-EYE VIEW: a perspective from the sky, or from an extremely high place

CENTERING: placing a subject in the middle of the frame

CLOSE-UP: an image made from very near a subject, often within touching distance

COLOR PRINT: a photographic image in color, usually made from a color negative or slide, most commonly on a paper backing

COMPOSITION: the organization of shapes, lines, tones, and colors

CONTEXT: the situation in which a subject is located

CROPPING: selecting only a portion of a negative or slide to be printed as the final image

DECISIVE MOMENT: an instant at which some part of an event's meaning is understood by a photographer and registered in an exposure

EXPOSURE: allowing light to strike the sensitive surface of the photographic film or paper; also, the amount of light allowed to do so

EYE LEVEL: the height of a creature's eyes

FILM: transparent plastic with a coating that is sensitive to light

FLASH: a portable light source, usually attached to or built into a camera

FOREGROUND: that part of the space in a scene or a photograph that's closest to the camera

FRAME: the border or edge of the photographic image

FRAMING: deciding where that border or edge will be placed

HAND CAMERA: a camera light enough in weight to be supported by the photographer's hands, without the use of a tripod

LENS: the glass "eye" that controls the amount of light entering the camera

LIKENESS: any image that resembles a particular person

MICROPHOTOGRAPHY: photography done through a microscope

MIDDLE GROUND: that part of the space in a scene or a photograph that's between the foreground and the background

MOTION PICTURES: movies

NEGATIVE: film that has been exposed to light by photographing; may be either black & white or color. The tones or colors of the scene photographed are reversed in the negative

PANNING: moving the camera in the direction the subject is moving during exposure

PHOTOGRAPHIC SEQUENCE: two or more photographs presented in a specific order

POINT OF VIEW: the position from which a photographer observes a scene

PORTRAIT: a photograph that suggests something about the individuality of a particular person or animal

POSING: presenting oneself deliberately as a subject for the making of a photograph

POSITIVE: a photographic image, usually a print, most often made from a negative on light-sensitive paper

PRESS PHOTOGRAPHER: a photographer who makes pictures for magazines and newspapers

PRINT: a photographic image, usually a positive, made from a negative; most commonly on a paper backing

SCALE: the relationship in size between two or more things

SHUTTER: the part of the lens that opens and closes, allowing light to strike the film

SHUTTER RELEASE: the button or other device that operates the shutter

SHUTTER SPEED: the rate at which the shutter opens and closes, usually adjustable by the photographer

SILHOUETTE: the outline of an object's shape, which is created by backlighting

SLIDE: a transparent image, usually in color, made to be viewed with a slide projector

SNAPSHOT: a photographic exposure made very quickly, most often with a hand camera

STROBE: a particularly powerful and rapid form of flash; may be portable or immobile

STUDIO: a space set up and reserved for an artist or photographer to work in

SUBJECT: the object or event the photographer is observing and describing

TELEPHOTO LENS: a lens that compresses space like a telescope, bringing distant events closer to the film in the camera

THREE-QUARTER PROFILE: an image of the head of a person or an animal, as seen from an angle halfway between the front and the side of the head

TRIPOD: a three-legged stand used to support a camera

VIEWFINDER: the small window in the camera body that allows the photographer to see what the lens is pointing at and framing.

VIEWPOINT: see *point of view*

VIGNETTING: leaving out everything in the image except the main subject

Credits